The Emerald Princess Plays a Trick

THE JEWEL KINGDOM

The Emerald Princess Plays a Trick

JAHNNA N. MALCOLM

Illustrations by Neal McPheeters

SCHOLASTIC INC.
NEW YORK TORONTO LONDON AUCKLAND SYDNEY

No part of this publication may be reproduced in whole or in part, or stored in a retrieval system, or transmitted in any form or by any means, electronic, mechanical, photocopying, recording, or otherwise, without written permission of the publisher. For information regarding permission, write to Scholastic Inc., 555 Broadway, New York, NY 10012.

ISBN 0-590-21287-7

Text copyright © 1997 by Jahnna Beecham and Malcolm Hillgartner. All rights reserved. Published by Scholastic Inc. LITTLE APPLE PAPERBACKS is a trademark of Scholastic Inc,

12 11 10 9 8 7 6 5 4 3 2 1   7 8 9/9 0 1 2/0

Printed in the U.S.A.   40
First Scholastic printing, August 1997

For Marie Van Valkenberg
and Her Princess, Lily

CONTENTS

THE JEWEL KINGDOM

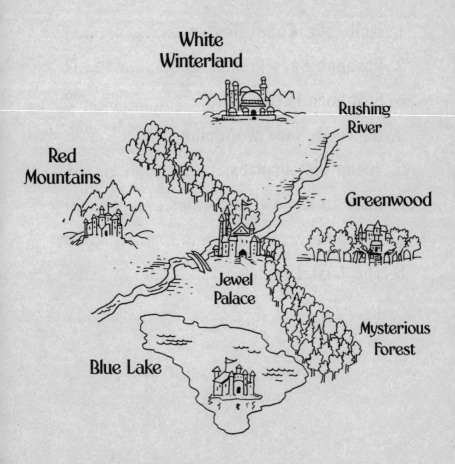

White
Winterland

Rushing
River

Red
Mountains

Greenwood

Jewel
Palace

Mysterious
Forest

Blue Lake

Emily the Court Jester

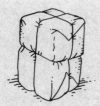Princess Emily slowly peeked around the trunk of the big elm tree. From where she hid, she could see Staghorn, the palace gardener. He was trimming the mulberry bushes that lined the path to her home in the Greenwood.

"Watch this," Emily whispered to her friend Arden, who stood a few feet behind her. "This is going to be *so* funny!"

Staghorn aimed his clippers at a small bush. Just as he snapped them shut, Emily tugged on the string she was holding. The bush leaped away from the dwarf.

"Hey!" Staghorn cried, nearly falling backward. "What's going on?"

Emily covered her mouth. Her green eyes sparkled. Her red hair shook with laughter.

Staghorn adjusted the glasses perched on the end of his nose. "My eyes must be playing tricks on me," he muttered.

He opened his clippers again, leaned toward the bush, and snapped the blades together.

Emily tugged on the string once more. The bush sprang in the air.

"Whoa!" Staghorn fell forward.

Emily couldn't help it. She burst out laughing.

"Hey!" Staghorn shouted, rubbing his nose. "What's so funny?"

Emily danced out from behind the tree.

Staghorn's face turned a bright red. "Princess Emily!" he cried, taking off his cap. "I didn't see you."

"Of course not, Staghorn," Emily giggled. She gave him a big hug. "I was hiding."

His furry eyebrows met in a frown. "Then it was *you* who made the bush hop away from me?"

"Yes!" Emily showed him the string she'd attached to the bush. "Wasn't that funny?"

Staghorn stared up at the Emerald Princess for a long time. "Yes, Princess," he said finally. "It was very funny."

Emily pointed at him. "You should

have seen the look on your face when the bush leaped in the air."

"I'm sure I looked very surprised," Staghorn said, brushing off the knees of his brown trousers.

"You looked positively silly!" Emily declared.

"I'm glad I made you laugh." Staghorn gestured down the path. "Now if you'll excuse me, Princess, I had better get on with my work. I have to do some pruning in the Twisted Vines."

Emily hugged the little man once more. "Thank you, my dear Staghorn. You are a very good sport!"

She watched the dwarf hurry off into the trees. Then she turned to Arden. "Wasn't that fun?"

The beautiful white unicorn blinked her big brown eyes. "I think it may have been fun for you, Princess. But I'm not so sure about Mr. Staghorn."

"Oh, he loves tricks," Emily said, picking a tiny bluebell and braiding it into Arden's mane. "Staghorn is like a grandfather to me. I've been teasing him since I was a little girl at the Jewel Palace."

Emily and her three sisters grew up in the Jewel Palace. It sat at the heart of the Jewel Kingdom. Her parents, Queen Jemma and King Regal, lived there.

"Did you see his face?" Arden asked.

Emily shrugged. "Staghorn always looks a little grumpy. That's why he's so much fun to play tricks on."

A bell chimed high above them. It came from the Emerald Palace, a magnificent tree house held up by six huge cedar trees.

On the tip of one of the pinecone-covered turrets sat a carved wooden clock. Emily had been given the clock by the people of the Greenwood when she was crowned the Emerald Princess.

Ding-ding-ding!

The clock chimed again.

"Did you hear that, Arden?" Emily asked. "It must be noon."

Arden turned her head. "Weren't you supposed to meet Princess Roxanne now?"

Emily's big green eyes widened. She covered her mouth with her hand. "I almost forgot! We're supposed to meet at the edge of the Greenwood."

Princess Roxanne was the Ruby Princess, and she lived high in the Red Mountains. Roxanne had been visiting Demetra, the Diamond Princess. Demetra was the oldest sister. She ruled the White Winterland.

"Arden, would you mind giving me a ride?" Emily asked. "We'll reach the border much quicker that way."

"Hop on, Princess." Arden ducked her head and bent one knee.

Emily hiked up her green velvet skirt and hopped onto the unicorn's back.

"I have a special surprise for my sister." Princess Emily patted the small package she held in her lap. "But I need to be at the border before Princess Roxanne."

"Surprise?" Arden asked as she cantered beneath the rustling leaves of the Greenwood. "What is it?"

Emily bent close to the unicorn's ear and whispered, "If I told you, it wouldn't be a surprise." She patted her friend's neck. "Now let's hurry, please!"

Arden broke into a gallop. She leaped lightly over a fallen log, then ducked under a low-hanging branch.

Emily threw her head back and flung her arms out to the sides. "What a wonderful day!"

Ahead, they could see bright light, where the Greenwood ended and the Rushing River began.

"Head for that big gray rock by the river," Emily cried as they burst out of the woods.

"What are we going to do there?" Arden asked.

"Not *we*," Emily said, jumping off Arden's back. "Me."

The princess unwrapped the bundle she'd been carrying and pulled out a black hooded cape. "Keep a lookout for Princess Roxanne, will you?"

The unicorn looked toward a dark line of trees cutting across the meadow. "I think I see her," Arden announced. "Coming out of the Mysterious Forest."

"Perfect." Emily slipped the hooded cape over her head. She darted behind the big rock. "Now hide yourself, Arden. I'm going to give my sister the surprise of her life."

"But, my lady . . ." Arden started to say.

Emily put one finger to her lips and pointed toward another rock across the clearing. Arden obediently trotted out of sight.

The Ruby Princess was hard to miss. Roxanne wore a red satin dress that flashed in the afternoon sun. A crown with one gleaming ruby rested on top of her jet-black hair. And on her arm she wore a bright red-and-silver shield.

Roxanne paused on the bank of the Rushing River and squinted toward the Greenwood.

"Not yet," Emily whispered to herself. "Wait. Wait. . . ."

Roxanne hopped across the Rushing River, following a path of smooth gray stones.

"Here she comes," Emily giggled.

Roxanne stopped to squeeze the water out of the hem of her dress.

"Almost." Emily bent her knees.

Roxanne took two steps forward.

Emily raised her hands above her head.

Roxanne turned.

Emily shouted.

"Boo!"

Roxanne Sees Red

"You scared me!" Princess Roxanne cried, once she realized it was Emily hiding beneath the cape.

"I know!" Tears of laughter rolled down Princess Emily's cheeks. "You screamed so loudly, *you* nearly scared *me!*"

Roxanne usually enjoyed a good joke. But this was not funny. Her dark eyes flashed and she stomped one foot. "Emily, stop laughing this instant!"

That only made Emily laugh harder.

"I was truly frightened," the Ruby Princess went on. "I thought you were a Darkling."

Emily slapped her knee. "Isn't that funny?"

"There is nothing funny about Darklings," Roxanne said, glaring at her sister. "They are our worst enemies."

The Darklings and their ruler, Lord Bleak, had been banished from the Jewel Kingdom years before. They now lived far across the Black Sea.

"It is a terrible sign when a Darkling appears in our land," Roxanne continued. "As a princess of the Jewel Kingdom you should understand that."

"I do," Emily said as she wiped the

tears from her cheeks. "But we can't worry about them *all* the time. We should be able to have some fun."

"Scaring people is not my idea of fun," Roxanne declared.

"Oh, come on!" Emily swatted playfully at her sister's shoulder. "Don't be a stick-in-the-mud. I play tricks on my friends in the Greenwood all the time. They love it."

Roxanne arched an eyebrow. "Are you sure?"

"Of course. Just ask Arden." Emily pointed to the unicorn, who stepped out from behind the other rock. "She'll tell you."

"Arden!" Roxanne cried happily. "I'm so glad you're here."

The unicorn bowed low. "Hello,

Princess Roxanne. It's a pleasure to see you."

"My sister and I are having a discussion," Roxanne explained. "She says the tricks she plays on everyone are funny. What do you think, Arden?"

Arden ducked her head and studied a small circle of pansies at her feet. "Well . . ."

"Be honest!" Roxanne advised.

"I think practical jokes are only funny to the people who play them," Arden finally said.

Roxanne put her hands on her hips and faced Emily. "See?"

Emily waved one hand. "That's just Arden. She's too sensitive."

Arden blinked her eyes patiently.

Emily hopped onto a moss-covered log

and carefully walked the entire length of it. "Tell me, sister, why are you in such a bad mood today?"

"You put me in a bad mood," Roxanne replied.

"Oh, fiddle!" Emily spun. "You know, I *had* planned a very fun afternoon for us."

"Doing what?" Princess Roxanne asked.

"First we *were* going to visit the fairies. They're making a cradle out of a walnut shell for Ivy's new baby."

"The baby has lavender eyes," Arden told Roxanne. "She's a beautiful fairy child."

Emily perched on a thick root. "Then we *were* going to have dewberry tea at the Emerald Palace. And after that, we *were* going to go for a swim at Looking-glass Pond."

"*Were?*" Roxanne repeated.

Emily sighed dramatically and tilted her nose up to the sky. "Now I'm not sure we should do any of those things. You are being such a grump."

"Grump!" Roxanne's jaw dropped open. "Emily, that's a very mean thing to say."

Emily shrugged. "I'm just being honest."

"No," Roxanne replied. "You're being impossible!"

Emily nearly fell off her log. "What?"

"And selfish!" Roxanne marched up to the log and put her face close to Emily's. "And I don't feel like spending another second with you!"

With a brisk nod to Arden, Roxanne

turned and marched out of the woods.

"Roxanne!" Emily cried, trying to get her balance. "Where are you going?"

"To the Blue Lake," Roxanne shouted over her shoulder. "To see Sabrina. I'm sure *she'll* be happy to see me."

Sabrina, the Sapphire Princess, was the fourth Jewel Princess. She lived across from the Greenwood in Blue Lake.

"Roxanne, please wait!" Emily leaped off the log and ran to follow her sister. "I was just kidding. I'm happy to see you. Come back!"

Princess Roxanne didn't even turn around. She marched straight across the Rushing River and kept going until she reached the edge of the Mysterious Forest. Then she turned and looked back at Emily and Arden.

"What's she doing?" Emily murmured.

Roxanne slowly raised the red-and-silver shield fastened to her right arm. She murmured a few words and vanished.

"Did you see that!" Emily gasped to Arden. "Roxanne used her magic shield so I wouldn't be able to see her. Why would she do — ?"

"Princess!" a new voice called.

Emily spun and watched as a young man stumbled out of the Greenwood. He wore a leather vest and a feathered cap. It was Crosscut, the young woodsman.

"Princess," Crosscut gasped, falling to one knee. "Come quickly. Staghorn is hurt."

"Staghorn the gardener?" Emily asked. "But I just saw him a short while ago. He said he was off to prune the Twisted Vines."

"Something went wrong," Crosscut

explained. "He got caught in the Twisted Vines and now he's in great pain. Please come quickly."

This was very serious.

"Thank you for telling me, Crosscut," Emily declared. "We'll go to him at once."

Staghorn Is Hurt!

 When they reached the Twisted Vines, Crosscut took Princess Emily and Arden to Staghorn. He was lying on his back beside the Babbling Brook. A fairy named Hazelnut was tending to his leg.

"Staghorn!" Emily cried, kneeling beside the little dwarf. "Where does it hurt?"

Staghorn turned his head away.

"It's his ankle," Hazelnut replied. "I think it's broken."

"Oh, dear!" Emily stood up. "We must get him the Emerald Palace immediately."

"No!" Staghorn cried out. "Not the palace. I want to go to see Nana Woodbine."

Nana was famous all over the Greenwood for her healing powers. She lived in a tiny cottage at the Heart-o'-the-Wood. Her mother had been half fairy, half wood sprite, and her father was a wizard.

"Nana is the perfect person to call," Emily told Hazelnut. "Let's bring Staghorn to my palace, and we'll send for Nana Woodbine."

"No!" Staghorn cried again. "I don't want to go to the palace."

"Go to Nana Woodbine's," Hazelnut said, fluttering above Staghorn's head. "You'll be safe there."

"Please, help me up!" Staghorn said, gesturing to Crosscut, the young woodsman.

Emily bent to help, but Staghorn shook her off. Crosscut gave the princess an apologetic shrug and helped Staghorn to his feet.

"How did Staghorn get hurt?" Emily asked Hazelnut as Crosscut and the dwarf hobbled away from them.

"Why do I need to tell you?" Hazelnut said rudely. Her wings buzzed as she hovered above Emily.

Arden pranced forward. "Because she is Princess of the Greenwood, and she has asked you a question."

Hazelnut scrowled. Then she perched

on a nearby limb and pointed across the brook. A rope dangled from the limb of a sycamore tree. "That rope caught Staghorn by the ankle and yanked him up to the treetops. Luckily the woodsman was here to cut him down."

"Poor Staghorn!" Emily gasped. "He could have hung there for a very long time!"

"But where did the rope come from?" Arden wondered.

"Ask the princess," Hazelnut said as she flew away. "*She* should know."

Emily was confused. No one in her kingdom had ever spoken to her that way before. She turned to Arden and asked, "What did Hazelnut mean by that?"

Arden touched Emily's shoulder with her horn. "Don't let her worry you, Princess," the unicorn murmured.

"Staghorn is the one who needs your concern. Let us go to Nana Woodbine and see if there is anything we can do to help the poor man."

"As always, you are right," Emily said, smiling at her friend. "Let's not waste another second."

4

Hurry to Nana Woodbine

Nana Woodbine's cottage was covered in ivy. Bright-red shutters framed the windows. Cheery clouds of smoke puffed out of the stone chimney.

Emily raised her hand to ring the bell. But before she could touch it, the door swung open.

"Welcome, Princess," Nana Woodbine

said with a sweet smile. "I knew you would come."

Nana was beautiful. She had delicate features and eyes the color of the ocean. Tiny flowers were woven into the braids circling the top of her head.

Emily peeked around Nana. She could see Staghorn lying on a carved wooden bed in front of the fire. He was surrounded by his Greenwood friends.

"How is Staghorn's ankle?" Emily asked.

"It isn't broken," Nana replied.

Emily heaved a sigh of relief. "Oh, thank goodness."

"But it is very badly bruised." Nana Woodbine leaned forward and whispered, "And so is Staghorn's pride. He felt like a fool hanging upside down like that."

Emily nodded. "I would have, too. May I see him?"

Nana frowned. "I don't think that's a very good idea. He needs to rest."

"But isn't there something I can do to help?" Emily asked.

"No, Princess," Nana replied. "I've rubbed his ankle with sneezewort and I'm just about to give him a spoonful of mercury vine. Now if you'll excuse me . . ."

Before Emily could say another word, Nana closed the door in her face.

Emily turned to Arden. "Something very odd is going on here. Why won't Nana let me talk to Staghorn?"

"I don't know, Princess," the unicorn replied. "But it is very strange."

Laughter erupted inside.

"I wish I were a tiny mouse," Emily

said, "so I could creep inside that cottage and hear what they're all saying."

"Why don't you use your magic pan flute?" the unicorn suggested. "The one that the great wizard Gallivant gave to you."

Emily's eyes widened. "My pan flute! But I've never used it before."

Arden smiled. "There's always a first time."

Emily wore the pan flute on a golden rope draped over one shoulder. "The high note will make me small," she said, remembering what the wizard had told her. "And the low note will make me tall."

Arden nodded. "That's right, my princess. But remember, once you are small, you must stay that way until sundown."

"I remember." Emily touched the flute

and felt a tingle in her fingertips.

"Are you ready?" Arden asked.

"I think so." Emily carefully raised the pipes to her lips. "Here goes."

The princess took a deep breath and blew the highest note possible.

There was a flash of light, and a loud whirring sound filled the air.

One second later, Emily found herself standing beneath a large mushroom. She was staring into the pink eyes of a little gray mouse.

Princess Emily and the mouse were exactly the same size!

Teeny Tiny Princess

"Shoo!" Emily shouted in the mouse's face. "Get away from me."

The mouse twitched his whiskers several times, then bared his teeth.

That made Emily very nervous. She grabbed a twig lying near the mushroom and waved it at the mouse.

"Go back to your home this instant or I'll . . . I'll bop you on the nose!" Emily cried.

The mouse curled its lips, but after a few seconds it scampered away.

"Phew!" Emily said, collapsing against the stem of the mushroom. "That was close."

Suddenly a big white furry thing loomed in front of Emily's face.

"Good heavens!" The princess instantly squeezed her eyes closed and covered her head. "It's going to get me!"

But all she felt was a gust of warm wind.

Emily cracked one eye open, then tilted her head back. The white furry thing was Arden's nose. And the warm wind was coming from the unicorn's nostrils!

"Princess?" Arden's voice boomed in Emily's ears. "Are you all right?"

Emily covered her ears and shouted back, "I'm fine, but it's a little scary to be so small. Even the tiniest mouse could hurt me."

"Why don't you let me pick you up with my teeth, and carry you to Nana's front door?" Arden suggested.

Emily looked at the unicorn's huge ivory teeth and gulped. One mistake and Arden could nip her in two!

"Don't worry," Arden whispered. "I'll be very, very careful. I'll only bite your dress."

Emily knew she had to trust her friend. "All right, Arden." She turned her back so the unicorn could grab hold of her skirt. "Lift me up!"

Arden carefully bit down on the emerald-green dress. Then she gently lifted the princess into the air.

"Whee!" Emily giggled, watching the ground zoom away from her. "I feel like I'm flying."

Arden walked ever so slowly up the stone steps to Nana Woodbine's front door and set Emily down.

"That was fun!" Emily giggled. "It was just like being at the tiptop of the Greenwood."

"I'll wait for you right here," Arden told the princess.

Emily saluted the unicorn, then knelt down and peered beneath Nana's door. There was just enough room for her to squeeze under it.

She crossed her fingers. "I just hope no

one steps on me when I get inside."

Emily flattened herself against the top step and wiggled her way into Nana's cottage. It was snug and warm and smelled of freshly baked bread.

"Mmmmm! Delicious!" Emily murmured as she straightened up. She tried to find Staghorn, but a pair of huge, worn boots blocked her view of the room.

Emily recognized the boots.

"Why, it's Fluke, the fisherman!" she said, stepping backward and looking up at the gray-bearded old man. "Word certainly travels fast!"

Fluke tended the Greenwood's brooks and streams. He and Staghorn were great friends. He must have run to Nana's when he heard that Staghorn was hurt.

"I'll hide under the bed where Staghorn is resting!" Emily murmured, inching her way along the wall. "That way I can see and hear everything."

Fluke, Hazelnut, and Crosscut circled the bed. They were listening to Staghorn tell a story about his old days at the Jewel Palace.

"Queen Jemma and King Regal always treated me like one of the family," Staghorn was saying. "There was many a time that I pulled all four of the Jewel Princesses around that garden in their little rainbow-colored wagon."

Emily couldn't help smiling. Those were fun times for her, too. She scurried under the bed, anxious to hear more.

"It would break Regal's heart if he heard how the Emerald Princess was treating the people of the Greenwood," Staghorn said.

"What!" Emily gasped from her hiding spot behind the bed leg.

Hazelnut fluttered onto the quilt and squeaked, "Just yesterday the princess nearly scared the stuffing out of the palace cook. Mrs. Dumpling's hands shook so much she completely ruined the cake she'd spent three hours decorating."

Emily winced. She had no idea Mrs. Dumpling was so upset.

Nana Woodbine sat on the edge of the bed. "I know this mercury vine tastes terrible," she told Staghorn, nodding at the wooden spoon in her hand. "But I want you to swallow it before you tell any more stories."

"Give it to Princess Emily!" Fluke

joked. "It would serve her right."

The group burst into laughter.

Emily could feel her cheeks turn a bright red. Her friends were making fun of her!

"I'll bet the princess has played a trick on everyone in the Greenwood!" Fluke declared. "She's played at least three on me."

"And this is the worst part," Hazelnut added. "We all have to pretend her jokes are funny, just because she's our princess!"

Emily shook her head. "Oh, no."

"I'm going to speak to King Regal about this," Fluke said, slamming his fist in his hand. "When a princess starts hurting her own people, then it's time for her to stop being a princess."

"They think I'm the one who trapped Staghorn!" Emily gasped.

It was too much to bear!

Emily's chin started to quiver and hot tears welled up in her eyes. *I have to get out of here,* she thought. *I have to run.*

Emily stumbled out from under the bed and headed straight for the cottage door. She didn't care if anyone saw her or even stepped on her.

Arden was waiting for the princess when she rolled out from under Nana's door.

"Oh, Arden, I'm so ashamed," Emily cried, burying her face in her hands. "You and Roxanne were right. No one liked my tricks. They only pretended that they did. Now they're all blaming me for Staghorn's injury."

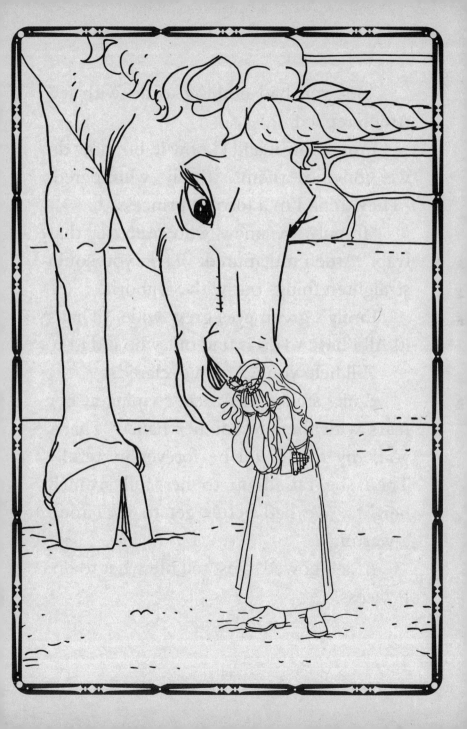

"But you had nothing to do with it," Arden replied.

"You know it and I know it, but how do we convince them?" Emily whimpered. "They think I'm a terrible princess."

"If only we knew who *really* set that trap," Arden murmured. "Then you could straighten things out with Staghorn."

Emily's green eyes grew wide. "That's it! All I have to do is find out who did it!"

"I'll help you!" Arden declared.

Emily smiled at Arden, swiping at her tears with the back of her hand. "Thank you, my friend. I'll be forever grateful." Then she raised up to her full six-inch height. "We had better get to it. Time's a-wasting."

Arden bowed. "Just tell me what to do, Princess."

Emily climbed down the stone steps of Nana's cottage. "I want you to take a message to Princess Roxanne. She's at Blue Lake. Ask her to join me as soon as possible."

"But where are you going?" Arden asked.

Emily raced through the tall blades of grass, slashing at them with a twig. "Back to the scene of the crime," she cried. "You'll find me at the Twisted Vines!"

Back to the Twisted Vines

 Emily bent over to catch her breath. It had taken her two hours to run to the Twisted Vines.

"If I weren't so small I would have been here ages ago!" she huffed, clutching her side. "Now I'm tired and very hungry."

She spied a blackberry bush on the path in front of her. Emily stood on tip-toe and reached for a big, ripe berry.

But something blocked her way.

At first she thought it was just a spider's web covered in leaves and twigs.

Emily carefully poked at the web. It was strong, like rope.

"Wait a minute," she murmured under her breath. "This isn't a spider's web, it's a net! But what is it doing here?"

Emily carefully lifted a blackberry leaf and peered through the netting. Underneath the net was a big, wooden cage.

"The trap is set!" a voice rasped above her.

Emily spun around and nearly fainted. She was staring directly at the biggest, ugliest feet she had ever seen. They were bony knobs with big tufts of fur on the toes and heels.

Slowly Emily raised her head. The feet

belonged to two creatures in long black capes and hoods. She couldn't see their faces, but she knew who they were.

"Darklings!" she murmured. "I can't let them see me!"

Luckily Emily was wearing green. She backed up against the leaves stuck to the netting, hoping to blend in.

"This cage will hold one very stout dwarf and maybe a few of his fairy friends," the other Darkling said in a crackly voice.

"That's good," the first one replied. "If we capture them two and three at a time, our plan will move much faster."

"Plan?" Emily gulped.

"These Greenwood folk will make good workers for Lord Bleak."

Emily's hands flew to her face. These awful Darklings were planning to kidnap her people. She had to stop them!

"But how can I do that?" Emily looked down at herself. "I'm just one person, and a tiny person at that."

Keeping as close to the ground as possible, Emily bolted through the grass to a hickory tree at the edge of the Twisted Vines. There she scurried up the trunk and hid in the crook of the first branch.

Below her the Darklings had finished setting their trap.

"I've got to warn my people!" Emily declared as she watched the caped figures hurry off to hide in the forest. "I need to find a Shinnybin."

The fastest way to get a message to anyone who lived in the Greenwood was to use a Shinnybin. They were sweet-faced creatures with extra long arms and legs.

A Shinnybin could climb to the top of

a tree in a matter of seconds. Once there, he or she used a system of clicks and knocks to spread the news through the forest.

Emily, who still had her twig, carefully tapped on the bark of the birch tree. Two slow knocks, three quick, and a whistle.

She was immediately answered by a *rat-a-tat!*, a whistle, and a shriek of delight, as a furry creature swung onto her limb.

It was the Shinnybin named Sorrel.

She blinked several times at the tiny princess, but asked no questions.

"At your service," Sorrel finally said. "What can I do for you?"

Emily wanted to tell Sorrel that two of Lord Bleak's Darklings had set the trap that hurt Staghorn. But she was afraid Sorrel wouldn't believe her.

"Please deliver this message to my

people," Emily said. "The Twisted Vines are dangerous. Stay away! What happened to Staghorn could happen to you!"

Sorrel flopped her long arm across her brow in a salute. "Got it! I'm on my way, Princess."

Suddenly the Shinnybin sprang to the next tree and shinnied to the top. Within seconds, Emily could hear the clicks and knocks of her message being sent across the treetops.

Princess Emily was about to follow the Darklings to their hiding place when she heard a voice singing below her.

"Me name is Fluke and me game is fish,
Ta-roll, ta-roddle, ta-rish!"

"Fluke!" Emily gasped. "He's headed right for the Darkling trap!" She cupped

her hands around her mouth and screamed, "Fluke! Look out!"

Fluke stopped walking and scratched his ear. "Eh?"

"Oh, dear," Emily murmured. "I'm too little for him to hear me." She climbed down the trunk of the tree until she was eye level with the fisherman.

"Fluke, look at the tree! It's me, Emily!"

The old fisherman turned his head. When he saw the tiny princess, he leaped backward. "Hey, what's going on here? Is that you, Princess?"

Emily shouted as loudly as she could. "Yes, it's me!"

Fluke leaned his face toward her. "But how did you — ?"

Emily waved one hand. "Never mind

about that! You're in danger. Don't go into the Twisted Vines."

A cloud covered the old man's face. "Is this another one of your tricks?"

"No!" Emily placed one hand on her heart. "I swear it!"

Fluke narrowed his eyes. "I don't believe you, Princess. I'm off to find an herb for Nana Woodbine. And I have to follow that path!"

He pointed at where the cage was hidden.

"No, please!" Emily cried. "It's a trap!"

"Sorry, Princess," Fluke replied. Then he swung his pack over one shoulder and marched toward the cage.

The princess didn't hesitate. She hurled herself through the air, landing on Fluke's shoulder.

"I can't let them catch you!" Emily

declared as the fisherman neared the trap. "They'll have to take me first!"

With a great heave, Emily leaped off his shoulder and flung herself at the netting.

Snap! The netting tightened around her.

Thunk! Emily dropped into the cage.

Whoosh! The cage, with Princess Emily trapped inside, was yanked up to the treetops!

7

Trapped!

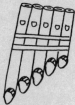 As Princess Emily swung back and forth in the treetops, Fluke looked up at her in dismay.

"Are you all right?" he shouted.

Emily pressed her face against the cage and called, "I'm a little bruised, but fine."

"Please forgive me, Princess!" the fisherman cried, clutching his hat to his chest. "I thought you were just playing another trick."

"Don't worry about that, Fluke!" Princess Emily shouted down to the poor fisherman. "We haven't time."

She knew the Darklings weren't far away. If she and Fluke didn't do something quickly, they both would be taken prisoner.

"Cut me down!" She pointed at the rope tied to her cage. "Hurry!"

Fluke reached for the knife on his belt and ran to the rope. It was wrapped around a big, wooden stake in the ground.

While Fluke sawed at the rope, Emily kept a lookout for Darklings. It was getting late and the sky had turned a pinkish color, which made it harder to see.

"Princess Emily!" Fluke called from

below. "My knife can't cut this rope! It's too thick!"

"Oh, no!" Emily could see the Darklings making their way through the trees.

"Forget about the rope," she cried. "Hide yourself."

"But what about you?" Fluke asked.

Emily looked up at the setting sun and began to think.

If the Darklings walked slowly enough, she might be able to save Fluke and herself.

"I have a plan," she cried to Fluke. "Now go hide!"

Fluke ducked into the bushes several yards from the trap while Emily stared at the sun. She held her breath, watching it slip slowly toward the horizon.

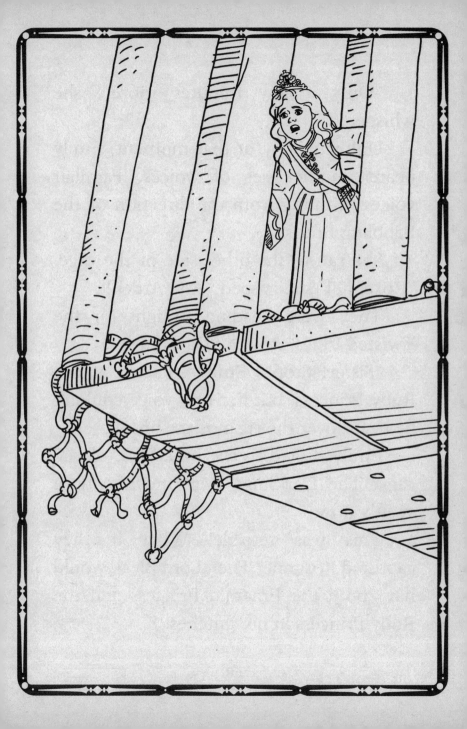

"Only a few minutes more," she whispered.

Unfortunately, at that moment, Emily heard another set of voices. Familiar voices. Coming from the direction of the Babbling Brook.

She ran to the other side of the cage. "Roxanne!" she gasped. "And Arden!"

They were heading straight for the Twisted Vines. And the Darklings!

"Sister! Stop!" Emily shouted at the Ruby Princess, but her tiny voice couldn't be heard over the rush of the brook.

Emily darted to the other side of the cage. The Darklings were moving more swiftly now.

This was terrible! What if they captured Roxanne? Then Lord Bleak would have both the Emerald Princess and the Ruby Princess in his clutches!

Emily felt for the pan flute at her waist as she looked back at the sun. "Hurry up and set!" she ordered.

Crack! A twig snapped just below her. The first Darkling had arrived at the trap.

He looked up at the cage and cackled. "Well, what have we here? It looks like we've caught ourselves a tiny . . ."

His voice caught in his throat as he realized his prisoner wasn't one of the fairy folk, but a real princess.

"The Emerald Princess!" the other Darkling gasped when he arrived. "But how did she get so small?"

Emily could feel her knees grow weak. They'd caught her and soon they would catch her sister. She looked back at the sun.

"Lower the cage," the first one ordered. "Let's have a look at her."

The cage jerked toward the Darklings.

But Emily never took her eyes off the sun.

The cage hit the ground with a thud. Emily reached one shaking hand toward her flute.

Arden and the Ruby Princess stepped out of the woods. "What have you done to my sister!" Roxanne cried.

The two Darklings turned, just as the sun disappeared below the horizon. "This is our lucky day!"

But then Emily raised the flute to her lips . . . and blew!

The Last Laugh

Bits of wood shot everywhere as Princess Emily burst out of the cage.

In an instant she turned from a six-inch princess into a giant as tall as a tree.

The Darklings screamed in fright. They turned to run.

"Not so fast!" Emily's voice boomed.

She grabbed the Darklings by their

hoods and lifted them over Roxanne and Arden. They dangled high in the air.

"Please don't hurt us!" the first one begged.

"I want you to leave my land, do you hear?" she roared.

"Yes, Princess," the second one cried. "Please just put us down."

Emily held them over a thorn bush. "Promise me you'll never come back."

"We promise!" the Darklings moaned.

"And if I ever catch you in the Jewel Kingdom again," she warned, lifting them higher in the air, "I'll turn you into teeny tiny bugs."

"No!" the Darklings howled.

Emily dropped them beside the Babbling Brook. The Darklings leaped across the stream and fled without ever looking back.

"Well, I guess we've seen the last of those two," Emily declared to Arden and her sister.

Roxanne had been speechless since Emily turned into a giant. Finally she gasped, "Emily, you were magnificent!"

Emily bowed. "Thank you, sister."

"Can you really turn people into bugs?" Fluke called from his hiding place behind a hollow stump.

Emily laughed so hard, her breath shook the tree branches. "Of course not. But they don't know that."

Roxanne stood on tiptoe and called, "What's the view like up there?"

"I can see everything," Emily replied. "The Emerald Palace, Nana Woodbine's cottage. Why, I think I've even spotted another one of those awful Darkling traps."

She leaned toward a red cedar growing almost ten feet away. Emily carefully tugged on something that looked like a vine. In an instant the trap sprang. Another cage just like the one that had caught her flew into the air.

"We must be sure to warn our people about these," Emily told Arden. "There could be more that I don't see."

Arden bowed. "Yes, Princess."

"Excuse me, Princess," Fluke said, inching forward. "I'd like to thank you for saving my life."

Emily touched the old man on the head with her fingertip. "It was nothing, Fluke. I would have done the same for anyone in my kingdom. I just wish they knew that."

"Don't worry, Princess," Sorrel the Shinnybin cried as she swung from her treetop to join the group. "I'll spread the word."

"And I will, too," Fluke added. "Sorrel and I will see to it that Staghorn and Nana Woodbine know who really set those traps. And who saved my life."

"Thank you both," Emily said with a smile. "I owe everyone in the Greenwood an apology, but first I must speak to my sister."

Emily knelt, so she could talk to Roxanne privately. "I've learned that my tricks only hurt people's feelings," Emily confessed. "And I want to apologize for scaring you today."

Roxanne grinned up at her sister. "Apology accepted."

Emily raised her right hand. "I won't ever do it again."

"That's the best news I've heard all day," Roxanne replied.

Emily stood up and clapped her hands. "Now what do you say we all go to my palace and celebrate?"

"And what's the special occasion?" Fluke asked.

"The end of Princess Emily's practical jokes," Roxanne declared.

"I'll celebrate that!" Arden cried.

Princess Roxanne tapped her sister's knee. "Emily, I'm getting a crick in my neck from looking up at you. Do you think you could change back now?"

Arden cleared her throat nervously. "Um . . . she can't."

"I can't?" Emily gasped. "Why not?"

"Once you've used your magic flute to change size, you must remain that way for another half turn around the sun," Arden explained.

"You mean I have to stay this way until morning?" Emily cried.

Arden nodded.

This tickled Roxanne so much she nearly fell over laughing.

"What's so funny?" Emily demanded.

"For once, dear sister," Roxanne giggled, "the joke is on you!"

Little by little, Princess Emily's frown changed into a smile. Soon she was giggling as hard as her friends. And the Greenwood rang with their laughter.

About the Authors

JAHNNA N. MALCOLM stands for Jahnna "and" Malcolm. Jahnna Beecham and Malcolm Hillgartner are married and write together. They have written over seventy books for kids. Jahnna N. Malcolm have written about ballerinas, horses, ghosts, singing cowgirls, and green slime.

Before Jahnna and Malcolm wrote books, they were actors. They met on the stage where Malcolm was playing a prince. And they were married on the stage where Jahnna was playing a princess.

Now they have their own little prince and princess: Dash and Skye. They all live in Ashland, Oregon, with their big red dog, Ruby, and their fluffy little white dog, Clarence.